The Giant and the Shoemaker

based on a Maltese folk tale

by Lynne Benton and Amerigo Pinelli

W

FRANKLIN WATTS

LONDON•SYDNEY

Conrad was a shoemaker. He travelled
from village to village mending shoes.
Sometimes people couldn't pay him
so they gave him gifts.
One day, when he had finished mending
their shoes, two villagers paid him with gifts.
The woman gave him some cheese and
the man gave him a little bird.
"Thank you," said Conrad.

Then Conrad noticed that the villagers

looked worried.

"What's the matter?" he asked.

"There's a giant in the forest," said the woman,

"and he's going to eat us."

"He has taken our mayor away already,"

said the man.

"That's terrible!" said Conrad. "Don't worry.

I'll find your mayor."

The Mayor

3

Conrad walked into the forest.

Soon he came across a big wooden cage.

Inside the cage, Conrad saw the mayor

of the village. He looked terrified.

An enormous giant stood next to the cage.

He had mean little eyes and big yellow teeth.

His legs were like tree trunks and he had

huge muscles. He looked very fierce.

The giant glared at Conrad. "What are

you doing in **my** forest?" he cried.

"I've come to rescue the mayor," said Conrad.

"No chance!" the giant said with a snarl.

"I shall eat him. Then I'll eat you, too!"

"Oh, no you won't!" said Conrad.

"I'm stronger than you!"

"Rubbish!" said the giant. "We'll have a contest.

And when I win, I'll eat you first."

"Fair enough," said Conrad. "Anything

you can do, I can do better."

The giant sneered. He bent down, picked up

a stone and crushed it in his fist until

it crumbled into dust.

"Can you do **that**?" he asked.

Conrad pretended to pick up a stone, but
he took the cheese out of his pocket instead.
He squeezed the cheese until it dripped water.
The giant frowned. "Water from a rock? How
is it possible?"

"But, surely you can't throw as far as I can!"

the giant said.

He picked up another stone and threw it

as hard as he could. It went up high

above the trees, then crashed back down.

"Beat **that!**" said the giant.

Conrad pretended to pick up a stone, but
he took out the little bird instead.
He tossed it high into the air.
The giant scowled as it flew higher and higher
and did not stop going up.

"But you can't do **this**!" the giant boasted. And he pulled a great big tree out of the ground, roots and all. He held it up proudly and stared at Conrad.

11

Conrad took out a rope and began

tying it between the trees.

"What are you doing?" asked the giant.

"Pulling up the whole forest," said Conrad.

"No, you can't," shouted the giant. "I live here!"

"Think of another contest, then," said Conrad.

"I know!" cried the giant. "We'll have
an eating contest. I will certainly win that!"

"All right," said Conrad. "What shall we eat?"

"Pasta," said the giant. "It's my favourite food,
apart from people."

"Fine," said Conrad. "Bring everything we need,
and we'll meet back here in an hour."

Conrad hurried back to the village and asked the villagers for a leather bag and a large overcoat.

"I need them to help me defeat the giant," he said.

The villagers ran to help him.

He fastened the bag round his belly and pulled the big coat over the top.

Then Conrad went back to the forest.

The giant was waiting for him. He had built

two fires. Two enormous cooking pots hung

over the fires. The giant boiled some water

and tipped a sackful of pasta into each

cooking pot.

Soon the pasta was ready to eat.

The giant gobbled his down so quickly

he didn't notice that Conrad slipped

most of his pasta into the leather bag

hidden inside his coat.

When both plates were empty, the giant said,

"See? I ate more than you!"

"No," said Conrad, "I ate more than **you**!"

"PROVE IT!" roared the giant.

"We'll count how many pieces of pasta

we each ate," said Conrad.

"How can we do that?" asked the giant, confused.

"Like this," said Conrad, grabbing a knife and slicing open his leather bag.

The pasta spilled out all over the ground.

"Right!" said the giant.

Then he grabbed the knife, sliced open

his belly...

... and fell down dead. Conrad unlocked

the cage and freed the mayor.

"Thank you!" said the mayor.

As they hurried back to the village,

the mayor shouted, "Come out, come out!

Conrad has killed the giant."

"Hooray for Conrad!" the villagers cheered.

Story order

Look at these 5 pictures and captions.
Put the pictures in the right order
to retell the story.

1

The villagers tell Conrad about the giant.

2

The village is saved!

Conrad tricks the giant.

Conrad and the giant eat pasta.

The villagers help Conrad get ready.

Independent Reading

This series is designed to provide an opportunity for your child to read on their own. These notes are written for you to help your child choose a book and to read it independently.

In school, your child's teacher will often be using reading books which have been banded to support the process of learning to read. Use the book band colour your child is reading in school to help you make a good choice. *The Giant and the Shoemaker* is a good choice for children reading at White Band in their classroom to read independently.

The aim of independent reading is to read this book with ease, so that your child enjoys the story and relates it to their own experiences.

About the book

A giant is terrorising a small village. Will the clever shoemaker be able to free the village mayor from the hungry giant and save the villagers from being eaten up?

Before reading

Help your child to learn how to make good choices by asking:
"Why did you choose this book? Why do you think you will enjoy it?"
Ask your child about what they know about giants. Then look at the cover with your child and ask: "Which person do you think is the shoemaker? Why"
Remind your child that they can break words into groups of syllables or sound out letters to make a word if they get stuck.
Decide together whether your child will read the story independently or read it aloud to you.

During reading

Remind your child of what they know and what they can do independently. If reading aloud, support your child if they hesitate or ask for help by telling the word. If reading to themselves, remind your child that they can come and ask for your help if stuck.

After reading

Support comprehension by asking your child to tell you about the story. Use the story order puzzle to encourage your child to retell the story in the right sequence, in their own words. The correct sequence can be found on the next page.

Help your child think about the messages in the book that go beyond the story and ask: "In this story, which talent proved to be more important, strength or cleverness? Why?"

Give your child a chance to respond to the story: "Which character was your favourite? Why?"

Extending learning

Help your child predict other possible outcomes of the story by asking: "What if the giant hadn't been tricked at the end by the shoemaker? How else might the shoemaker have convinced the giant to move away and stop terrorising the village?"

In the classroom, your child's teacher may be teaching different kinds of sentences. There are many examples in this book that you could look at with your child, including statements, commands, exclamations and questions. Find these together and point out how the end punctuation can help us understand the meaning of the sentence.

Franklin Watts
First published in Great Britain in 2020
by The Watts Publishing Group

Series Editors: Jackie Hamley and Melanie Palmer and Grace Glendinning
Series Advisors: Dr Sue Bodman and Glen Franklin
Series Designers: Peter Scoulding and Cathryn Gilbert

A CIP catalogue record for this book is
available from the British Library.

ISBN 978 1 4451 7218 7 (hbk)
ISBN 978 1 4451 7223 1 (pbk)
ISBN 978 1 4451 7229 3 (library ebook)
ISBN 978 1 445 1 7927 8 (ebook)

Printed in China

Franklin Watts
An imprint of
Hachette Children's Group
Part of The Watts Publishing Group
Carmelite House
50 Victoria Embankment
London EC4Y 0DZ

An Hachette UK Company
www.hachette.co.uk

www.reading-champion.co.uk

Answer to Story order: 1, 3, 5, 4, 2